For my daughter, Paige, who can see just fine.

My heartfelt thanks to Cecily Kaiser and Meagan Bennett, for making the process of creating this book such a wonderful experience.

Special thanks to David R. Stager Sr., MD, and Kenneth Berk, OD, for their optical expertise.

Library of Congress Cataloging-in-Publication Data

Barclay, Eric, author, illustrator.
I can see just fine / Eric Barclay.
pages cm
ISBN 978-1-4197-0801-5
[1. Eyeglasses—Fiction. 2. Vision—Fiction.] I. Title.
PZ7.B2357Iaj 2013
[E]—dc23
2012048270

Text and illustrations copyright © 2013 Eric Barclay
Beethoven image on pages 7 and 29 © Can Stock Photo Inc./Nicku
Book design by Meagan Bennett

Printed and bound in China
10 9 8 7 6 5 4 3 2

For bulk discount inquiries, contact specialsales@abramsbooks.com.

ABRAMS
THE ART OF BOOKS SINCE 1949
115 West 18th Street
New York, NY 10011
www.abramsbooks.com

I CAN SEE JUST FINE

Eric Barclay

Abrams Appleseed
New York

One day at school, Ms. Palmer noticed that Paige was having trouble seeing the chalkboard.

Mr. Thompson noticed that Paige was having trouble reading her sheet music.

Dad noticed that Paige was having all kinds of trouble.

I found a kitty!

But when anyone asked Paige about her eyesight, she would always say:

The next morning, Mom told Paige that she didn't have to go to school that day. Paige was excited!

But Paige was NOT excited when Mom told her they were going to see the eye doctor instead.

Paige was a little nervous when they arrived at the doctor's office.

I
CA
NSE
EJUS
TFINE
EDFCZP
FELOPZD

1
2
3
4
5
6
7
8

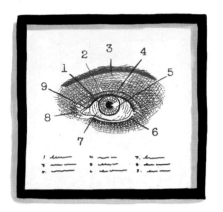

The Human Eye

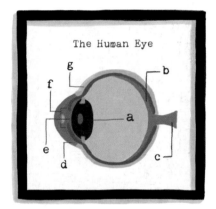

But Dr. Steiger was very nice. He asked Paige to read some letters on an eye chart.

Dr. Steiger put some special drops in Paige's eyes,

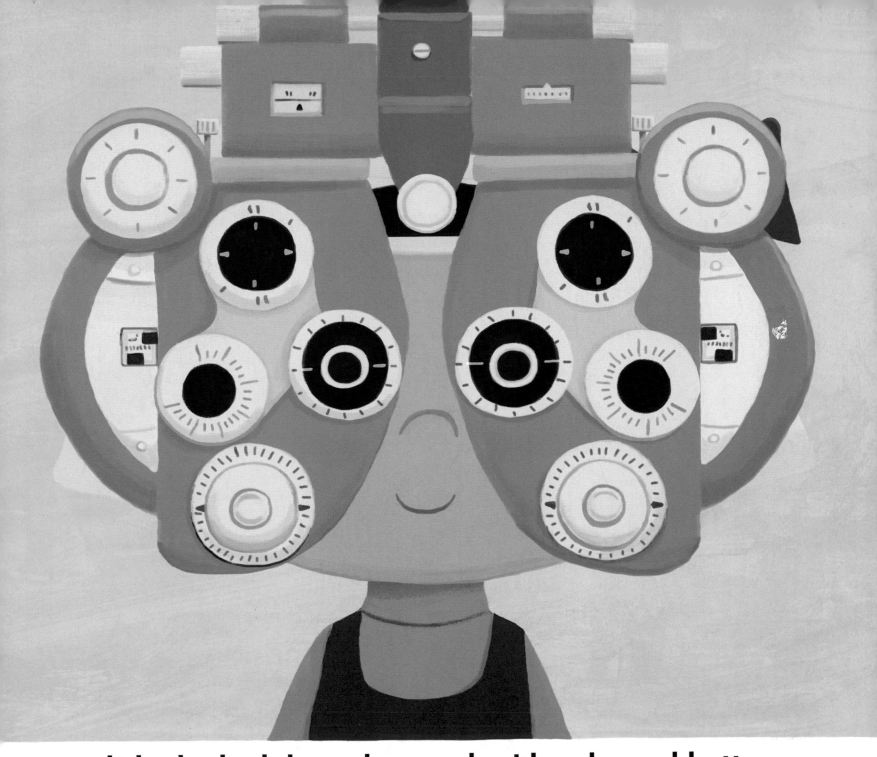

and she looked through a mask with nobs and buttons.

When they had finished, Dr. Steiger said, "Well, kiddo, you need glasses. But don't worry, they'll look great on you!" Paige was not pleased.

Mom and Paige went to pick out some eyeglass frames.

Paige tried on lots and lots of different frames . . .

. . . until she found the pair that looked just right.

After a couple of days, Paige's glasses were ready. "Let's try these on, Paige," the lady said.

"But I don't need glasses," Paige said. "I can see . . ."

". . . EVERYTHING!"

After that, Ms. Palmer noticed that Paige had no trouble seeing the chalkboard.

Mr. Thompson noticed that Paige had no trouble reading her sheet music.

Dad noticed that it was time to get Paige a kitty.

I found a skunk!

And mom noticed that Paige's new glasses were all smudged.

"Your glasses are filthy! There's no way you can see out of those!"